♥A Woodland Wedding♥

Read more
OWL DIARIES
books!

OWL DIARIES

♥ A Woodland Wedding ♥

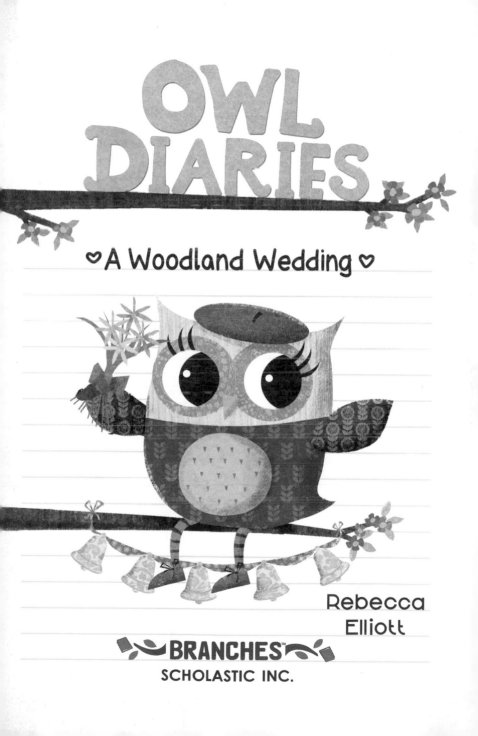

Rebecca
Elliott

BRANCHES

SCHOLASTIC INC.

For Benjamin. My youngest owlet. — R.E.

Special thanks to Eva Montgomery.

Library of Congress Cataloging-in-Publication Data

Elliott, Rebecca, author.
A woodland wedding / by Rebecca Elliott. — First edition.
pages cm. — (Owl diaries ; 3)
Summary: Eva's teacher, Miss Featherbottom, is getting married, but when her special necklace disappears, Eva and her friends set out to track down the thief and return the necklace before the wedding.
ISBN 0-545-82557-1 (pbk. : alk. paper) — ISBN 0-545-82558-X (hardcover : alk. paper) — ISBN 0-545-83586-0 (ebook) — ISBN 0-545-83587-9 (eba ebook) 1. Owls—Juvenile fiction. 2. Teachers—Juvenile fiction. 3. Theft—Juvenile fiction. 4. Weddings—Juvenile fiction. 5. Elementary schools—Juvenile fiction. [1. Owls—Fiction. 2. Teachers—Fiction. 3. Stealing—Fiction. 4. Weddings—Fiction. 5. Schools—Fiction.] I. Title. II. Series: Elliott, Rebecca. Owl diaries ; 3.
PZ7.E45812Wo 2016
[Fic]—dc23

2015011353

ISBN 978-0-545-82558-0 (hardcover) / ISBN 978-0-545-82557-3 (paperback)

11 10 9 8 7   16 17 18 19 20

Printed in China   38
First edition, January 2016

Book design by Marissa Asuncion
Edited by Katie Carella

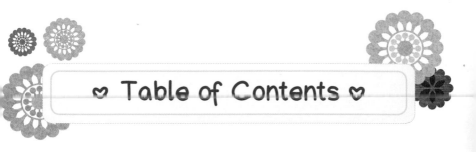

♥ Table of Contents ♥

♡ Hello There! ♡

Sunday

Hello Diary,
   I'm back! It's ME — Eva Wingdale!
I wonder what fun we're going to have
together this week!

I love:

Painting

Writing to-do lists

The smell of strawberries

My pillow

Reading mysteries

The word <u>lollipop</u>

Bluebells
(my favorite flower)

Laughing with
my friends

I DO NOT love:

My brother Humphrey's LOUD guitar playing (He's good, but he's so NOISY!)

The word <u>swamp</u>

Sue Clawson (when she's mean)

Brushing my feathers

Rainy nights

The smell of
squirrel poop

Mom's worm cake

Seeing anyone
feeling sad

I totally LOVE my family!

Here we are on vacation in sunny
OWLIFORNIA:

Dad

Humphrey

Me

Baby Mo

Mom

My pet bat, Baxter, is part of my family, too.

He's so sweet!

Owls do all sorts of cool things — like fly SUPER fast.

We stay awake ALL night.

We sleep in the daytime.

And we see things really far away with our BIG eyes.

I live at Treehouse 11 on Woodpine Avenue in Treetopolis.

My best friend is Lucy Beakman.

Lucy lives next door! We talk on our **PINEPHONES** all the time.

Lucy has a pet lizard named Rex. Rex is Baxter's best friend. We love dressing up our pets!

Lucy and I go to school together. Here is a photo of our class:

Miss Featherbottom

Sue   Kiera   Zara   Macy

my class

Zac George Me   Lucy Jacob   Lilly Carlos

It's almost sunrise. I need to go to sleep. Talk to you tomorrow, Diary!

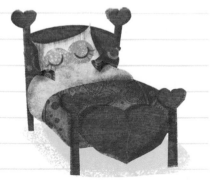

♡ A Mystery Owl ♡

Monday

Miss Featherbottom told us some very exciting news tonight.

Tomorrow is Pet Day. That means you can bring your pets to school with you!

How **FLAPERRIFIC** is that, Diary?! I can't wait for everyone to meet Baxter!

We drew pictures of our pets.

Kiera drew the best picture. So she got to ring Barry the Bell. We all love ringing Barry the Bell.

We were getting ready to fly home when we saw a handsome OWLMAN waiting outside for Miss Featherbottom. They started smiling at each other, and then they stood wing-in-wing!

Treetop Owlementary

We wondered who the owl might be . . .

Everyone giggled.

Lucy came over to my tree house after school. We talked about Miss Featherbottom's mystery friend.

I hope he IS her boyfriend.

They looked so happy together!

They really did! But now we need to stop chatting and get on with planning tomorrow's Pet Day!

Should we dress up our pets?

Yes! And why don't we decorate Rex's and Baxter's cages, too?

That's a flap-tastic idea, Eva!

We dressed up our pets as kings. And we turned their cages into castles — to match their king costumes. We even decorated their castles with sparkly jewels!

I can't wait to meet everyone's pets! Sleep tight, Diary!

♥ Pet Day ♥

Tuesday

Today was **FLAPPY-FABULOUS**, Diary!
The pets were ALL cute!

Flash:
Jacob's giant snail

General Slithers:
George's snake

Sid:
Zac's spider

Steve:
Lilly's moth

Clive:
Carlos's goldfish

Rex:
Lucy's lizard

Baxter:
Eva's bat

Susan Wilkinson:
Zara's crab

Wilber:
Macy's tree frog

Gumdrop:
Kiera's bumblebee

Lady:
Sue's tortoise

And guess what! Because Rex's and Baxter's costumes looked SO great, Lucy and I got to ring Barry the Bell!

Bing-a-Ling-a-Ling!

At lunch, our class had a Pet Picnic. We ate **BUG BURGERS** and **FLY FRIES** and we gave our pets critter treats, blueberry chews, and saucers of milk!

Then Miss Featherbottom had <u>big</u> news to share . . .

The friend you saw me with last night is Mr. Plumage. He is my boyfriend. And we are getting married THIS SATURDAY!

You're ALL invited to the wedding! And because your pets have been so good today, they're invited, too!

YAY!

How exciting!

Flaperrific!

Please quiet down. I need your help, owlets. A <u>tradition</u> is something that's always done. And one wedding tradition is that the bride – that's me – has to wear <u>something old</u>, <u>something new</u>, <u>something borrowed</u>, and <u>something blue</u>. I already have my something old . . .

Miss Featherbottom took a beautiful necklace out of her desk drawer. It was super shiny, with beautiful jewels!

This belonged to my grandmother. It's <u>very</u> old!

Now I need you to help me come up with the rest of the items. What could I wear for something new, borrowed, and blue?

We called out ideas.

You could get a <u>NEW</u> feathercut?

You could <u>BORROW</u> my shoes? But they might not fit.

You could paint your feathers <u>BLUE</u>?

Flap-tastic suggestions! Thank you! Okay, time for your Winglish lesson.

I went to Lucy's house after school. We made wedding dresses from old sheets. And we dressed Rex and Baxter as grooms!

But then Sue Clawson flew by and said something REALLY mean.

You two look more like crazy ghosts than brides! Why are you playing weddings anyway? Weddings are SOOO squirrelly!

This is why sometimes I call Sue "Meany McMeanerson." How could anyone think weddings are squirrelly? Sue might not like weddings, but I LOVE them!

Now I'm off to bed to dream of my perfect wedding dress. Sweet dreams, Diary!

♥The Secret Wedding Club♥

Wednesday

I got to school super early today.
I did not want to miss <u>anything</u> Miss
Featherbottom said about the wedding!
But when I got to class she looked sad.

What's wrong?

Nothing really. I'm just worried because Saturday is soon and there's a lot to do for the wedding!

I felt sorry for Miss Featherbottom. I really wanted to help her.

At recess we all played weddings.
Well, all of us except for Sue. She
wanted to play jump rope games and
got mad when no one wanted to play.

My game is much more fun
than your stinky wedding game!

Then Meany
McMeanerson flew
off in a flap.

All during recess I kept worrying about Miss Featherbottom. Then I had a great idea! I called everyone over . . .

I'm going to start an after-school Secret Wedding Planners Club! We'll plan wedding things to help Miss Featherbottom. Who wants to join?

Great idea, Eva!

I'm in!

Sounds fun!

I'll join!

Me, too!

No, thank you. I have more important things to do.

After school our club had our first meeting. We wrote a wedding to-do list.

1. Bake a cake

2. Make decorations (garlands, balloons, tablecloths)

3. Pick flowers for the bouquets

4. Find a band

Next, we all flew to my house, picking flowers as we went. (I always pick bluebells!)

Then we made an **OWLSOME** cake!

And we had a flour fight!

I need to wash my feathers and get to sleep. There's still so much to do. But we should be fine — so long as nothing goes wrong tomorrow. And I'm sure nothing will go wrong. Right?!

♡ The Missing Necklace ♡

Thursday

Disaster! When we got to school Miss Featherbottom looked <u>really</u> sad.

Class, I have bad news. My special necklace – the <u>something old</u> that I was going to wear at my wedding – is missing!

The Secret Wedding Planners Club held an emergency meeting at my tree house after school.

We became the Secret Wedding Planners and Detectives Club! I've read LOTS of mystery books. So I knew we needed to do three things: dress like detectives, ask questions, and look for clues. We put on our detective outfits.

Then we flew back to school. Luckily, Miss Featherbottom was still there. Kiera started asking questions.

When did you last see your necklace?

I'm not sure exactly. I remember having it in my desk on Tuesday because it was Pet Day. And I remember General Slithers crawling through it. But I can't remember if I saw it after that.

Has anything else gone missing?

Well, now that I think about it, I couldn't find my silver star stickers or glitter pens this morning.

Next, we searched for clues. Zara pointed to Miss Featherbottom's desk.

Miss Featherbottom

Look at these scratch marks! Isn't this the drawer where the necklace was kept?

Yes. But the necklace isn't in the classroom anymore. And neither is the thief. Let's go search the forest.

No one paid much attention to the scratch marks. But I felt like I had seen them before. I just had to remember where!

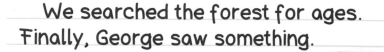

We searched the forest for ages.
Finally, George saw something.

Who's that over there?

It's Sue.

Look!
Her bag has
something shiny
sticking out of it!

And Sue doesn't
like weddings!

Maybe <u>she</u> took
the necklace!

We flew over to Sue.

What's in your bag, Sue?

None of your business.

Did you pick up Miss Featherbottom's necklace — maybe by mistake? Do you maybe have it in your bag?

I am not a thief, Eva! I didn't take the necklace!

Sue looked upset as she flew away. I felt awful. Oh, Diary! I guess I said the wrong thing? I was only trying to solve the mystery!

The club flew back to my house. We couldn't solve the mystery tonight, but we could work on other items from the to-do list.

Carlos and George blew up balloons.

Kiera and Zara picked flowers.

Lucy and I made garlands.

My brother Humphrey told us we were squirrel-heads for getting so excited about a wedding.

But we all got a lot done! And we had a **HOOT**! We couldn't wait to show Miss Featherbottom tomorrow!

After the other owlets left, I asked Lucy about Sue . . .

Lucy really is the best friend in the whole **OWLIVERSE**. I promise to apologize to Sue AND solve the case tomorrow!

♥ Meany Mystery Solved! ♥

Friday

Lucy and I flew over to Sue's house before school. I picked more flowers on the way – you can never have too many bluebells!

But, Diary, you'll never guess what we saw through Sue's window!

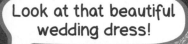

We knocked on the door. When Sue answered, she was covered in white silk. It looked like <u>she</u> was wearing a wedding dress!

42

Sue showed us the wedding dress.

Well, my mom is a fashion designer. She's making Miss Featherbottom's dress, and I've been helping her. When you saw me in the forest I was carrying my mom's sequins and sparkly thread.

Oh. Um. That's why we're here . . . I wanted to say I'm sorry for thinking you took the necklace.

That's okay.

Sue started to cry.

Sue and I made the flower crown while Lucy helped Sue's mom with the dress. The flower crown really looked WING-CREDIBLE – and so did the dress!

Miss Featherbottom smiled when we got to class.

This is a flaperrific surprise! I cannot believe your club made my cake, tablecloths, flowers, and garlands!

(We didn't show her the flower crown or the balloons. We had to keep some surprises for the wedding day!)

Poor Miss Featherbottom.

At lunch, we had an emergency club meeting.

Just then, my brother Humphrey
walked over.

> Hey, Eva, do you need a band? My band,
> <u>The Hootles</u>, could play if you want.

> Wow, Humph – that'd be amazing!
> Nothing too noisy though!

> Of course not.

Then he winked, which worried me.
But still – YAY! We found a band!

We flew to tell Miss Featherbottom the good news.

Then our newest detective took a look around the room. She opened Miss Featherbottom's desk drawer—the one below the scratch marks.

Sue used her magnifying glass to take a closer look.

After school, our club made another list. (I love making lists.)

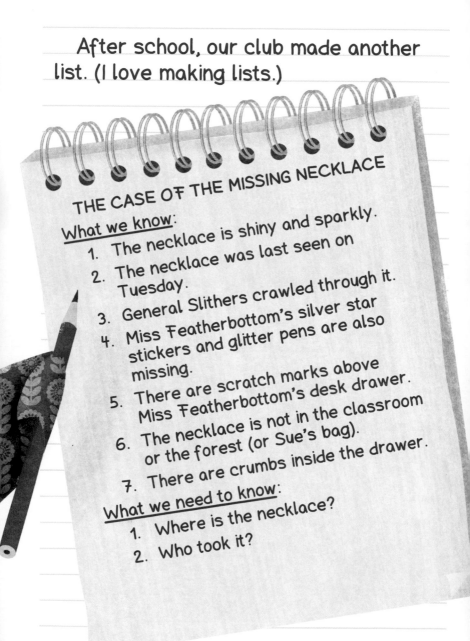

THE CASE OF THE MISSING NECKLACE

What we know:
1. The necklace is shiny and sparkly.
2. The necklace was last seen on Tuesday.
3. General Slithers crawled through it.
4. Miss Featherbottom's silver star stickers and glitter pens are also missing.
5. There are scratch marks above Miss Featherbottom's desk drawer.
6. The necklace is not in the classroom or the forest (or Sue's bag).
7. There are crumbs inside the drawer.

What we need to know:
1. Where is the necklace?
2. Who took it?

Diary, the wedding is <u>tomorrow</u>! We must solve the mystery! I'm going to think about the clues as I fall asleep . . .

♥ A Woodland Wedding ♥

Diary, today is THE day!! Do you like my dress?

Oh, and I THINK I KNOW WHO TOOK THE NECKLACE! But I won't say anything yet. We both know  I've been wrong before, and that didn't go well. I need to make sure I'm right before I even tell <u>you</u> my idea.

First, I need to phone Lucy.

Lucy and I flew to the wedding super early to set up. The other club members met us there.

Everything looks flap-tastic!

But we still haven't found the necklace.

Don't worry! Eva thinks she's solved the mystery!

Yes! I think—

Just then, Miss Featherbottom flew in.

Wow, Eva! How did you solve the mystery?
Teamwork! The crumbs Sue found made me sure the thief was a pet. The scratch marks Zara found made me think of Rex. Whenever Rex plays with Baxter he leaves scratch marks all over the tree.
I also know Rex likes shiny things! So I thought he must have taken the necklace, stickers, and glitter pens – all to decorate his castle!
Thank you so much, everyone!

Oh no! I was so worried about my necklace that I forgot my something new, borrowed, or blue! I don't have ANY of those things!

Sue and I looked at each other. We both had the same idea!

We can help you with that!

We handed Miss Featherbottom the flower crown we had made.

> It's new, it's blue, and — if you give it back — it's borrowed, too!

> Wow! Thank you so much! And it makes me hootingly happy to see you two working together.

Miss Featherbottom flew off to change into her wedding dress.

My dear Diary, the wedding was the most beautiful wedding I have ever seen! (Well, it was also the ONLY wedding I have ever seen! But I can't imagine a lovelier one!)

Later, we all danced to Humphrey's band.

Sue's mom came over and gave me an invitation to a <u>surprise</u> birthday party tomorrow – for Sue! She didn't forget!

We danced the day away, Diary! Now I must get some sleep! I can't wait to see Sue's face when she finds out about the surprise tomorrow!! Good day!

♥ Surprise! ♥

Sunday

Lucy, Kiera, and I flew to Sue's house early to help set up for the party. Other owlets were there, too. (Sue was out having lunch with her dad.)

We reused some balloons from the wedding.

And we painted a birthday banner.

Sue's tree house looked beautiful. Soon, we heard Sue flying up. We hid just as the front door opened . . .

Then we all jumped up!

A woodland wedding and a surprise party in one weekend! <u>Phew!</u> This has been an amazing week, Diary! I can't wait until next week!

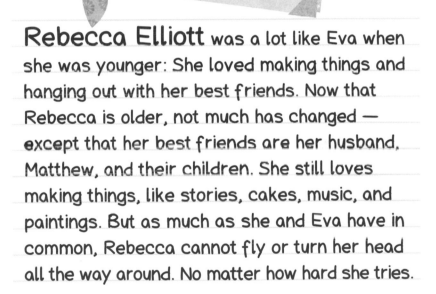

Rebecca Elliott was a lot like Eva when she was younger: She loved making things and hanging out with her best friends. Now that Rebecca is older, not much has changed — except that her best friends are her husband, Matthew, and their children. She still loves making things, like stories, cakes, music, and paintings. But as much as she and Eva have in common, Rebecca cannot fly or turn her head all the way around. No matter how hard she tries.

Rebecca is the author of JUST BECAUSE and MR. SUPER POOPY PANTS. OWL DIARIES is her first early chapter book series.

OWL DIARIES

How much do you know about A Woodland Wedding?

Planning a wedding is hard. What do my friends and I do to help Miss Featherbottom?

Miss Featherbottom's necklace is very special. Explain why the necklace is so important to her.

Eva loves reading mystery books — and she learns from them as well! What does Eva learn about how to be a detective? How does Eva use what she learned to solve the mystery of the missing necklace?

Why am I the only owl who is not super excited for the wedding?

Write a diary entry about a party you've attended. Explain the reason for the party, describe the decorations, list the guests, and add any other fun details!